VERSES KINDLER PUBLICATION

YOU, ME & MIKKI

Verses Kindler Publication

VERSES KINDLER PUBLICATION

Verses Kindler Publication.

Website: www.verseskindlerpublication.com

You, me and Mikki
By: Mrs. Radhika K Walia
ISBN: 978-93-5605-662-6

NON-FICTION STORIES 1st Edition
Price: INR 349/ $18

Disclaimer

You, me & Mikki is written by Radhika K Walia.

The published work is the original contents of the author and she has done her best to edit and make it plagiarism-free.

The characters may be fictitious or based on real events but they are not meant to hurt anyone's feelings nor portray anything against any caste or system. Any resemblance of names of actual person, place or institute is purely coincidental to carry forward the story.

In case of any plagiarized write-up, the author is solely responsible for it, the publisher would not be responsible for it.

VERSES KINDLER PUBLICATION

The book is written with love.

So, if you come across any error, skip it with love!

So, this is what soul laid bare feels like!

In the tumultuous year of 2021, I found myself facing a condition that bore an eerie resemblance to dementia. Yet, unlike true dementia, my affliction didn't stem from neurological degeneration. Instead, it was labeled "Pseudodementia"—a term that sent shivers down my spine.

For me, true dementia or not, my condition terrified me. Imagine waking up each day, uncertain if your memories would slip through your fingers like sand. The thought of not being able to hold my memories close to me, or even having an easy access to it on a quiet morning, or while on a walk, or a silent night, or preparing for festivities was scary.

Hence, You, Me & Mikki! Even as I pen down these words my heart swells with a mix of vulnerability, gratitude, nervousness, and excitement. This collection of memories, experiences, and my attempt at "adulting", is more than ink on paper – it's a piece of my soul laid bare. Each chapter, each sentence, represents a step toward learning and acceptance.

For years I've carried these stories within me, like fragile treasures hidden in the recesses of my heart. Stories that would have not got its meaning without the two constants in my life: Manav and Mahu—my anchors, my partners-in-crime. My forever.

Where Manav has always been my ground where my roots have grown more from his strength, my daughter—has been my silent gardener. Through her, I have come to learn that parenting isn't just about "raising" a child – it's about evolving alongside them. It's about witnessing their growth unfold before our eyes. Recognise the transformative power of love in parenthood. I learned to rise alongside her, dusting off my knees and getting on the ride again. The joy of playing with cardboard boxes, splashing in puddles of water, smelling spices, watching sunsets, following butterflies. She helped me refocus to find the extraordinary not in the ordinary, but in simple.

Both of them are my biggest strength—the reason I dared to write these pages. And open my life for everyone to know. My daughter's innocence, her curiosity—they've nudged me toward accepting my vulnerability as my strength. Her resilience mirrors my own, and her unwavering belief in magic reminds me that life is a tapestry of both shadow and light. She has a huge part to play in getting the book together as a bond between hearts. So before I started to mixing incidents, or getting confused with memories, I felt an ache in my heart to write these down and find solace in the 'universe'. Because for me the scariest thing is to not know, or remember these wonderful moments one day.

Life isn't always neat or linear, it's beautiful in its messy, imperfect way. Just like you, a guardian or a parent, I find my joy of parenthood in growing up with my daughter.

And remember, sometimes the bravest act is to let our stories breathe—to release them into the world, hoping they'll find their way home.

So, dear reader, as you turn these pages, know that you cradle my heart.

Thank you for being part of this journey.

Contents

Chapter One: If You're Happy and You Know It

The heart and soul of this story is Mikki.

Mikki is love and affection, maturity beautifully blended with innocence, and sensitivity much beyond her age; she's an old soul in a new vessel.

But who is Mikki?

Imagine a classroom where children are singing along to the catchy nursery rhyme, 'If you're happy and you know it, clap your hands!' The entire class is thoroughly enjoying; giggles and laughs, cheers and claps have filled the air. But there's that one small girl, sitting in the corner with a sad look on her face, unable to join in the celebration.

Even in such a happy place, that girl and whatever was holding her down would likely never be noticed…by most people. But, not Mikki!

Mikki is the one who notices the unnoticed. She will always notice that one person who could be feeling invisible in a group. She will make it a point to walk up to that one person with a warmth like mellow sunshine; flash her radiating smile; and speak kind words with innocence as pure as the unblemished and white hues of soft snowflakes.

She is the one who will say, "It makes me happy to see you happy! Please smile, and come to sing and dance with us!"

Enjoying the carefreeness of her 'tween' years and ready to take a step across the threshold toward being a teenager, Mikki is, at the same time, similar to and yet so different from any other child in this tender age.

She is vivacious and full of life, like a burst of enthusiastic energy in an otherwise dull world. She is curious to learn and eager to acquire new experiences.

And most of all, she is a fan favorite; beloved by all due to her endearing charm and pleasing personality.

She adores ladybirds, and when asked why, her quick response is, "Because they play on the fingers and listen to our wishes." Like her favorites, she too has a magical way of understanding what people wish for, be it a helping hand or a sounding board for their difficulties. And she too flits around like a gentle fairy, tugging on people's heartstrings, and making everyone come along on the joyride and fun adventure of life that she has embarked upon.

What sets her apart is her sensibilities; her compassionate and empathetic heart and mind full of wisdom, and her maturity that goes miles ahead of her years.

She is the best daughter that anyone could hope for, a fierce friend who is a great companion for the enjoyable times and the challenging ones, and an eager student for lessons taught by schools and life in general. She carries the strength in her to say "No" and stand up for what she values and holds close to her heart; something that does not come even with age to many others.

Young as she may be, she is also a great teacher for those intentional learners who are willing to see the world through her lens and dive into the treasure trove of learnings held in her experiences.

It is not one aspect or one life-defining moment that has made her the person with the heart of gold that she is today. It is a culmination of all the small measures over the years; the kind of environment created at home, the nature of interactions with people, the lessons taught at the right time. The essence of a child is developed from all these moments and it is the mould in which their personality eventually sets.

And who is responsible for shaping this mould? What is the primary learning system for children? What helps them distinguish between right and wrong, honest and dishonest, good and bad?

It is, of course, their parents and the values imparted to them in their early years.

Their young brains are akin to sponges, soaking in and absorbing everything they see and hear around them. They have an easy yet elegant way of understanding and perceiving things.
And Mikki's parents, realizing this at the very initial stages of their upbringing, fed her with all the right inputs which she then took, upgraded, and transformed into something beautiful. They created a safe spaces for her, and she refined the output with her unique and wondrous traits.

Take 'love', for example. As adults, we can try to articulate what the complex concept of 'love' stands for. While our understanding as adults may be more nuanced, a question to answer is that is such a deep approach really required, or do children do it simpler, but better? As Mikki understood it, the concept for her became as simple as her mother cradling her in her lap. She observed the special smile that came on her father's face when she made puppy eyes while longingly holding out her arms to be picked up and thrown in the air by him. For her the joy she felt when he scooped her up, caught her playfully and hugged her with a big smile was the feeling of love.

For 'caring', Mikki began to associate it with the tears she saw in her mother's eyes whenever she was ill or in pain, or when her father snugly tucked her into a warm sweater and socks to shield her from the cold.

They were small occurrences that left a big imprint. Through these incidents, Mikki observed, learned and started embodying these concepts in her own way. She realized the things she could do to show her love, care, affection and so on for people, and that's what she went on to do.

Much like sunlight, air, and water make a tiny sapling grow into a tree that delights everyone with the sight and scent of beautiful and fragrant flowers, the efforts and attention put while raising a child give way to a pure-hearted person who makes others happy.

Just like you, Mikki's parents did everything they could and led by example while doing so. Through their actions and interactions, they taught Mikki the most important values like showing up, compassion, gratitude, and resilience among others that became a deeply ingrained part of her personality and guided her through life. But it is one thing to understand and remember the teachings of parents. Right? Like a curious learner, Mikki embraced those teachings with open arms and made them her own. She gave it her own colours. Pink. Dark pink. Glitter pink. Through her own mindset, viewpoint, and understanding, she elevated those lessons and crafted them into a powerful and blazing guiding light for not just herself, but for those around her too. Like a ray of positivity and virtues, she illuminated and touched many lives with her innocent yet intelligent thinking.

Let's embark on this journey together. Mikki's stories will warm your heart, and make it smile. You will be able to see yourself in her wins and struggles. Most importantly her growth and above all remind you of the wholesome It will offer new perspectives, broaden imaginations, and above all, open up a potli of heartwarming and wholesome moments wrapped up in the weaves of sweet memories, under the comforting shade of the trees where the ladybirds and butterflies rest…

After all, if Mikki can embody great values with her yet-growing knowledge of the ways of the world, what is stopping us all?

Chapter Two: Whiskers & Wingbeats

Mikki was, and remains, a blessed child. Loving parents, a roof above her head, and warm food on her plate; these are the very basics that anyone needs to live a good life. But, she also has something much more that indeed makes her blessed and special in this world where selfishness, malice, and jealousy have sadly planted their poisonous roots and spread their venom.

Mikki thrives in this world and has the power to fight back these negativities, and this power stems from her heart that beats with kindness and compassion.

We have all heard these terms, and we often throw them around like confetti in conversation. But, have we ever stopped to think about whether we are simply using them as talking points, or whether we have gone a step beyond to truly embrace them? These are more than just values; they carve the path for a new and enriching way of life. They occupy a reserved space in our core personality and character, and they get seamlessly woven like threads of soft silk into our very essence. Once they make home there, they never leave us. But, it is mostly this process of making kindness and compassion a way of life that people struggle with.

Kindness is difficult to explain, but very easy to feel and discern. It is what makes one care for others, want to do good things for others, and find inner happiness in making others happy. The beauty of kindness can be compared with the scenic patterns of ripples formed on the surface of still water when a pebble gently bounces on it. A kind act indeed benefits the people directly involved in it. But it spreads its warmth and radiance to countless others too, creating a positive domino effect.

Compassion too is a nuanced concept, but at the same time, it is the simplest concept for it entails nothing more than feeling for others. It entails finding happiness in their joy, having their troubles and griefs resonate within you and fueling a desire to help in any way possible, and connecting with them on a more profound level.

Did Mikki take special lessons to understand these deep concepts? Did she go through any rigorous training to learn how to embody these values? How then did they start manifesting in her from as early as the age of 6 years?

It is because she saw and experienced these around her. In her little way, she made sense of the acts that she came to associate with kindness and compassion, and the positivity that it sparked in others. She subconsciously decided, without knowing the magnitude of the decision she had made at that young age, that she wanted to adopt and exhibit these traits. It conditioned her mind to react and respond in a certain way, and this set her up to be a kind and compassionate person.

And that's exactly what she went on to become and act like in every walk of life.

Story 1: Small Gestures; Big Impacts

It was a warm summer evening when Mikki, aged 6, returned home after playing badminton with her friends in a nearby park. Her mother, like usual, waited near the door to welcome her in with a hug and a smile, when she noticed that Mikki had not returned alone. In her small arms, she cradled 2 squabs. Usually, her gait was bouncy and fast, and she used to come racing ahead to leap into a bear hug with her mother. However, a sudden switch was made when she knew she had to take care of those creatures, and her mother observed in awe as she carefully walked forward, smiling down at the squabs, and telling them in a gentle tone, "I've got you home!"

She went up to her mother with a beaming grin and proudly showed off the squabs. When her mother asked about why she had got them home, Mikki replied, without missing a beat, "They didn't have their mummy. So I got them home for you to become their mummy and take care of them."

Mikki's mother was stunned into silence, for she could not believe that her young daughter was displaying such immense empathy, sensitivity, and thoughtfulness that could very rarely be seen in grown-ups. She asked for the whole story, and as her young daughter recounted the events, her surprise kept growing.

Mikki and her friends had been engrossed in their game when suddenly, she had been distracted with some sounds from a tree next to them. Ever inquisitive and keen to learn about the happenings of the world around her, Mikki had crept up to the tree to see a pigeon flying away and leaving behind the remnants of a nest that held her babies. Mikki's beautiful and expressive eyes had grown larger as she had stared at the sight, and her mind quickly drew an association that since the mummy had flown away, the babies needed a new mummy. Her friend, in a reaction more commonly seen for that age, had observed the spectacle for a few seconds and her interest had then wandered back to their game. Mikki however, had been unable to stop looking at the squabs. She had looked keenly up at the sky and craned her neck to see whether the mummy bird was returning. When she had seen no signs of the bird, however, her face lit up, for she had found the perfect solution. Afterall, when her mother had to step out to work, there were days that she spent evenings at her friend's house. And Aunty always took great care of her till her mother returned.

"Like you are my mummy, I thought you only could become their mummy too," she excitedly told her mother.

It is only human nature to be possessive about the things one possesses or the people one holds close; or is that only something we say to convince ourselves that our tendency to be selfish is an inbuilt trait that cannot be eliminated?

Mikki was at the age of seven where for children, their mother is the start and end of their world, the center of their universe. And yet, she had selflessly chosen to share her mother with 2 other creatures. At that moment in the park, she had chosen to tread a path that only held wonderful things for the people brave and good enough to take a step on it. She had chosen to exhibit kindness and compassion.

In the days that followed the squabs' arrival at their home, she ably rose to the occasion and helped her mother take care of them. In her mind, she perhaps became a 'big sister' to the baby birds. She became an eager little helper to her mother in whatever was needed to tend to the squabs. She gave her old shoe boxes to make a small bed for them, gathered cotton, and gently layered it in the box. Mikki took to herself to make the shoe boxes a snug home for her new friends. The boxes deserve their own special mention because Mikki loved collecting them; and yet, when the time came, she did not think twice about giving away her prized possessions. She constantly ensured that the birds were comfortable, neither feeling hot from the blazing sun nor cold from the air conditioning at home, and even started reading to them because she thought they might be bored without any of their family or friends there. When she returned from school every day, she first ran to see the birds and chuckled in delight as they cooed at her.

She had bonded so strongly with them that Mikki's mother feared how she would take it when the birds would inevitably fly away. She tried to prepare her daughter for it and gradually started telling her about how the birds are growing strong under her care. Letting her know how eventually the birds would want to return to their home in the trees and find others like themselves. Mikki, her small face displaying an adorable seriousness, pondered over what her mother said for a few seconds and then asked, "How do you know this mummy?" Her mother told her, in a way that was easily understandable for her young mind, that the pigeons' place in the world was not in their house. They needed the open air, lush trees, and free skies.

Mikki bobbed her head up and down at the explanation, and once again, took her mother by surprise when she said, "Ohh, I understand now! I would not be happy living in trees, just like that, they will not be happy in our house." It was clear that her maturity and ability to think from the shoes of another were racing ahead of her age.

The day that was expected yet dreaded arrived a fortnight later, once the birds had grown enough in size and strength. Mikki sat in the living room along with her parents, when suddenly, they heard a loud flutter of wings and saw the pigeons fly away through an open window in a flash of grey and black hues. Mikki's parents exchanged glances with each other, for though they had tried to prepare her for this first exposure to loss, they knew she would need their support to get through it.

Their daughter, however, looked at them with a wide smile and glowing eyes and started excitedly jumping in the air while clapping her hands. It was such a beautiful sight, for she radiated pure joy.

Her reaction was the best that anyone could hope for, and yet, her parents had no idea what had brought it on. The answer she gave to their question complimented her core personality; it was full of innocence and a magical imagination that made the difficult situation pleasant and much easier to handle. "They would not be able to fly away till they were fully strong again. So, I know we took good care of them and made them into big, strong birds!" she happily replied.

Mikki's parents, rightly, had been seeing the situation only from their daughter's perspective. They thought that for her, it spelled a number of complicated and challenging emotions like loss, her efforts into caring for the birds being met with rejection, or perhaps even a sense of betrayal upon them flying away. But Mikki only saw it from the perspective of the birds. She spun a new story in her mind, one that shone with positivity. She cared only about the fact that the birds were healthy enough for flight and was content in the role she played in achieving this. Being sad for herself never occurred to her; it was only happiness for them.

This feeling, that not every situation needs to be about oneself, is the foundation of compassion. It takes people years and years to master, and even then, their first instinct is usually to think about themselves. The magic of childhood is that there is inherent goodness in every tiny heart and mind. It just takes proper guidance and upbringing to keep this magic alive, which can go on to transform the whole world into a better place.

Story 2: Paws & Promises: The Furry Friend 'Shifu'

In another incident, that occurred during the years of Covid-19, Mikki once again touched lives with her kind actions. The family living next door to them had contracted the virus and they had asked Mikki's family to look after their pet. Shifu was an adorable ball of fur and bundle of affection whom Mikki had known and loved right from his puppy days. Once, after she had learned about the festival of Raksha Bandhan, she made up her mind to celebrate it with Shifu. She made a special rakhi for him, decorated the house with his favorite toys, and tied it to him to mark their new relationship. They indeed made the most heartwarming sibling pair ever!

When Mikki first heard of this new proposed arrangement, she said, "Aunty and uncle will recover much faster if they know Shifu is safe with us." Once again, her own delight took second place in her thoughts compared to the comfort and peace it would bring to Shifu's parents.

Mikki did everything possible to keep Shifu happy when he shifted in with her. "I think he will really miss his home and parents, so I want to spend all my time keeping him company," she said.

And so, Mikki read him her school books and used to giggle with joy when he wagged his tail at her exciting narrations. She kept him on her lap whenever she attended online school and lovingly stroked his head; he too would nuzzle against her palm and fall asleep many times. Mikki never liked to disturb his sleep and so, she would continue sitting still on the chair long after her school was over till Shifu woke up. Besides these fun parts, she took complete responsibility for the other aspects like feeding him on time, taking him for walks, and cleaning him. She made a special chair for Shifu with soft blankets and pillows so that he too could sit with them for lunch and feel included in their family.

When the time came for him to return, she hugged him tightly and wept at night, partly wishing that her mother would not hand him over. When she eventually let go, she said, her voice thick with tears, "I only had him for a few days and I am so sad about him going away. I know that is his home and he must be missing his Mumma and Papa." With this, she bid a bittersweet goodbye to Shifu, till she was back at his doorstep a few days later to resume their fun games with his favorite toy - a raggedy cushion!

It did not always have to be any momentous occasions that brought out these qualities, for they were always there within her. The way she sprinted to get her father a glass of water when he looked tired without him even having to ask for it, or the way she kept her own needs aside and first shopped something for all her loved ones while on a holiday, or the way she spent several hours of her day studying with her classmate who had missed a lot of the syllabus due to an illness; her kindness and compassion were highlighted equally in these small and daily occurrences.

They were, and continue to be like a bright light that casts an angelic glow around her. Whatever she may grow to become, and how many ever milestones she may cross in her education and career, she has already won her crowning glory. These traits are what stay with a person and not only enrich their lives, but of those around them too in perpetuity. Nothing can be compared to the immense power they wield, for it is everlasting.

Mikki's parents too find their ultimate solace in the fact that whatever else may come and go in her life, her kindness and compassion will forever be in bloom.

Chapter Three: Dandelion Whispers & Wishes

The renowned American missionary Edwin Cole once said, *"Maturity comes not with age..."* Mikki came to this world many decades after these words were immortalized, but it sure seems like she somehow influenced them. And like an inseparable companion that guided her through every challenge in life, it firmly held her hand and stayed with her.

The beauty of intangibles, like maturity, is that they can be felt even though they cannot be seen. One cannot look at a person and immediately realize they are mature, for it does not cast any special glow or put a person under a golden spotlight. But, after mere seconds of interaction, the inner maturity breaks past the external boundaries and shines forth.

And what makes this particular trait even more unique is the myriad of ways in which its benefits are felt. Mikki's maturity undoubtedly helped every person that she interacted with in some way or the other. For her friends, it helped them see their problems in a different light and tackle them. For her parents, it became a beacon that showed them the way through dark patches, and most importantly, became a testament to how well their daughter had imbibed their teachings.

However, her maturity also immensely helped Mikki herself. It cleared her mind from the mist of uncertainty that often doesn't let one see the clear picture and pushes them to make hazy and haphazard decisions. It served as an internal compass that always pointed her in the right direction. It taught her to differentiate between assertiveness and aggression, thereby empowering her to accommodate the interests of others without being a pushover. It was the gentle hand that supported her as she tried to fight her own battles, and the comforting voice that whispered self-assurances into her ears when she found her own solutions to problems. It was the magical key that opened up a treasure trove for her, and adorned her with the lovely jewels of confidence, sensibility, and rationality. The latter part of Edwin Cole's famous quote talks about what, if not age, it is that determines someone's maturity. According to him, it is the acceptance of responsibility. And it was the same according to Mikki's parents too, for it was the foundation upon which they developed maturity in their daughter.

As a small girl barely learning the new words that she longed to flaunt and adjusting to all the wondrous things she saw around her, Mikki could not have been given sermons about maturity and responsibility. She probably would have blinked her big eyes in confusion, and cocked her head in that heartwarming way that children do when they don't understand something.

But right from that age, being given the task of planning one meal for herself taught her these concepts very well. Or as she grew up a bit more, her involvement in family decisions taught her that she too could influence things in their household and hence had to put thought into whatever she suggested. The small chores they kept aside for her, like laying the dinner table or helping her mother organize their home, instilled accountability in her, and maturity developed as a wonderful by-product of it. When she saw her parents like become children themselves, versus having them quickly spring into adulthood when the situation demanded it, she learned the delicate balance between having fun and knowing when to take things seriously. When she saw them deep in conversation, she understood that clear communication helps in every situation. Without even realizing it, opening up to her parents about her joys and sorrows, achievements and failures became second nature to her.

Although, while embracing the highly adult-like quality of maturity, did Mikki grow up before her time? No! She never stopped being a child, and embodying the carefreeness that comes with it. She simply became a wiser, and more capable and understanding version of herself.

If maturity brings about such wonderful outcomes, why is not every one of us striving to inculcate it within ourselves? Why do we let ourselves get swept away with petty thoughts, rash decisions, and impulsiveness? That remains one of the greater mysteries of the world.

But Mikki has her sights on what is important- making maturity her best friend, keeping it close to her heart wherever she may go, and together making the correct choices to enrich her own life and those around her!

Story 3: The Unsaid Emotions

Mikki's father, as a requirement of his job, had to travel a lot. For 7-8 years, Mikki's mother did her best to slip into the role of both parents for her daughter. Mikki, too, small as she was, did everything in her power to ensure her mother felt supported through these ups and downs. Despite being away, Mikki's father never let her feel that he was not around. Right from ordering tasty treats for her as a surprise and asking about every small detail of her day every day, his heart was always with them.

Mikki's parents wanted to shield their daughter from the pain that these long periods of separation were bound to bring, despite feeling it themselves. However, they were unaware that their daughter understood their vulnerability very well. She heard the unsaid emotions, and felt the unexpressed sadness. Picture her like a small detective in a trench coat with a magnifying glass in her hand; she kept picking up and making sense of the subtlest of hints. She would catch emotion in her father's voice as he said "bye" on their phone calls, or the longing look in her mother's eyes upon seeing a family photograph. Mikki pieced these clues together to make sense of the story unfolding before her and determined a course of action for herself that she thought would be in everyone's best interests.

It was Daughter's day and Mikki's father had sent across a bouquet of flowers in her favorite color of shades of pink and a treat from Starbucks (her favorite Hibiscus Iced Tea). She had squealed in delight when the packages had arrived home; with beaming eyes and a smile that could melt even the coldest of hearts, she had asked her mother to call her father. She talked endlessly with her father, sharing every detail of her school, studies, and friends. Her father, too, eagerly awaited these calls, and filled her in on his own enthralling tales. Mikki's mother watched from afar as she clutched to the phone like it was a lifeline, and kept adding more and more discussion topics.It was like Mikki was fighting hard to keep hearing her father's voice and did not want the call to ever end. It was extremely sad yet extremely beautiful. As much as they wanted to avoid it, both sides eventually knew that it was time to end their conversation. With as much resolve and strength as she could muster in her young heart, Mikki gave a loud and hearty giggle, for she knew her father loved hearing her laugh, and kept the phone away. In the next instant, large teardrops welled in her eyes and she hurriedly ran away to her parent's room. Mikki's mother was shocked; she saw her daughter transition from cheery laughter to sorrowful tears within seconds.

Mikki had run toward her father's things, for those lifeless belongings held memories that could let her relive happier times. She ran her hand lovingly over the desk where he sat and worked, and opened his cupboard to gaze at the belongings he had left behind. She stayed like that for several minutes, and Mikki's mother watched her silently. When Mikki realized her mother too had joined her, she looked away from the cupboard with a broad smile pasted on her face. Mikki's mother had dearly hoped that her daughter would continue crying; that smile felt like a deeper blow to her heart than Mikki's tears.

She held her daughter close and gently said, "It is okay to cry in front of me; you don't have to be brave. I know you miss papa a lot."

Mikki bit her quivering lip and slowly replied, "I want to be brave because I know you both are doing a lot to make this easier for me. You are doing all the things with me that papa did, like taking me out to different places. And even papa, I know he is busy and still he spends so much time talking to me every day. I don't want to cry and make you both sad."

During such emotionally distressing times, it is always assumed that parents are the ones who need to take care of children, and never the one way around. But here was Mikki, suppressing her emotions to keep her parents happy. She had an understanding deeper than perhaps any other children would have about what her parents were doing for her, and she too wanted to reciprocate by going the extra mile for them. In an age where, naturally, the child's thinking is geared toward expressing their own emotions, Mikki maturely guarded her true feelings so as to prevent her parents from feeling more pain than they were.

Mikki asked, in a soft voice, "Aren't you and papa also just being brave for my sake? You both also never talk about how bad this situation is, or how much you miss each other. I just learned to do the same thing…" she said and trailed off.

But, she need not have said anything more, for Mikki's mother immediately understood the message she was trying to convey. Mikki had correctly identified the root cause of the struggle they were all going through and just as easily had provided a solution for it too. Mikki's mother ruffled her hair and affectionately said, "You're right, we all need to express ourselves more openly."

And with her innocent wisdom and maturity, Mikki opened lines of communication for her family. Small as she was, she brought about a big change. Expressing one's sorrow did not necessarily have to mean making others sad too; instead, she made the whole family share their pain, find strength in one another, and overcome it together. She showed her parents how important it is to feel the emotions, revel in them, and then let go. She taught them that it's important to be responsible for one's own feelings, because home is a safe space.

Story 4: The Student Becomes the Teacher

Mikki's mother, was a regular volunteer at her company's Corporate Social Responsibility events. For this particular event she was tasked with conducting a session on 'Good Touch, Bad Touch' in a school for underprivileged children. She worked hard to create a Power Point presentation including all the things that she felt were right; explanatory videos, relatable examples, and all the works. She discussed all this with Mikki, for her parenting style had always laid heavy emphasis on including her daughter in daily things. Her thought was that if Mikki learns that it's easy to appreciate each other's world, she will find it easier to open up and have a sense of comfort to let her parents in when she grows up. Also, because her mother knew that Mikki would give her a different lens to look at things, which she appreciated a lot.

In the midst of her mother's explanation, Mikki suggested, "Why don't you do your actual presentation in front of me? Exactly like how you're planning to do there. It will be good practice for you." Mikki's mother enthusiastically agreed for this. She had worked hard on it, for she wanted to make a significant impact on the youth. She excitedly started with the presentation, but barely 5 minutes into it, Mikki shook her head and said, "You need to change this!"

Her mother was stunned. She asked Mikki what was wrong; whether she was going too fast or slow, whether it was too simple or complicated. Mikki simply said, "You're not teaching these things to your team, or to children like me who are lucky enough to have parents like you. You need to present it in a way they can understand and remember."

Mikki then went on to elaborate her own experience in school. She explained how their entire batch felt awkward and uncomfortable, and that the children her mother would be interacting with would find it even more difficult to hear about these things. Mikki's mother was relieved to have taken her daughter's coaching on this matter; like always, she had given a unique perspective to things. When she was asked for her suggestions on how the presentation could be made better, Mikki thought deeply and presented some excellent ideas.

"You can use a swimming costume to help girls understand about their private parts, without making them feel embarrassed. It will be better to learn this way for boys too. And most importantly, you should tell them what to do in case they face any bad situation. I know I can just come running to you and papa, but sadly they don't always have that option. That should be the main focus of your session."

Mikki's mother heard her out with rapt attention. She could not believe that her young daughter, a student herself, was teaching her such important concepts with such maturity. She hurriedly got to work and Mikki sat up with her the whole night to recreate the presentation, and offered many more wonderful tips.

As they finished, sleep heavy on both their eyes, Mikki quietly asked, "Did you feel bad, mumma? I know you had worked very hard on your presentation, I didn't mean to pick faults in it. I just wanted to help you do the best."

Mikki's mother looked tenderly at her, and said, "Of course I didn't feel bad. You're my daughter, but you're also my biggest teacher. And you taught me so many wonderful things today that are going to help others too."

Mikki gave a delighted smile and tightly hugged her mother. Her advice made her mother's session a big success. Not only could she resonate with the problems the children faced, but she taught them how they seek help for themselves. When Mikki's mother told her about this, she danced with pure joy, for she knew she had made a real difference.

Many others might have hesitated to criticize something that a loved one had put so much effort into. And perhaps, being so young themselves, they would have let inhibition hold them back, just blindly believed that the elders have got it right, and not voiced out their opinions on serious issues. But Mikki's inherently developed maturity made her choose a different path than what others would have. She reasoned that though her mother might have felt bad, she needed to hear the truth that would only help her going ahead. And though it was a subject usually reserved for discussion among grown-ups, Mikki was confident enough to put forth her thoughtful views.

Decision-making in challenging moments like this comes easily for a mature mind. Instead of meandering and getting lost amidst the endless possibilities and their potential outcomes, a mature mind can see things as they are.

And it is this mature mind of hers that will always look out for Mikki and become the anchor that stabilizes her against the waves and tides of life's uncertainties.

Chapter Four: The Brave Firefly

When she was a small girl, Mikki and her mother had once encountered a policeman climbing up a large tree. Mikki watched in awe as the policeman launched himself into the air, swung strongly from the branches, and eventually reached where he wanted – to a spot high up where an adorable kitten had somehow gotten stuck. He gently picked up the kitten, safely got her down, and handed her over to another delighted young girl who was the kitten's owner.

Mikki had tugged on her mother's kurta and signaled her to come closer. When Mikki's mother had leaned down close to her daughter, Mikki had excitedly whispered, "He's so brave; I want to be just like him when I grow up!"

Perhaps Mikki will grow up to join the police force and she too will one day rescue some little girl's pet. But, as of now, she ended up as an overachiever, for she fulfilled her goal of becoming brave before she even fully grew up!

A lot of adults too would associate 'bravery' with the same kind of imagery that sparked Mikki's interest in that value. A strapping policeman climbing a tree, a muscular hero fighting against villains, or a burly firefighter rescuing people from a burning building.

But we rarely link this term to the picture of a small and innocent girl who chuckles away in delight at the varied wonders of life, throws around joy and happiness on others like confetti, and speaks the sweetest and most pleasant words. However, within this same girl, there is a fierce and resilient warrior. While she usually loves to please others, she won't think twice about going against someone if they are wrong. While she usually delights everyone with her soft-spokenness, she won't hesitate to be firm with her words if it is for a good cause. And it is these acts that truly comprise bravery.

In this fiercely competitive and fast paced world, where everyone is looking to get ahead and falling behind is simply not an option, challenges and obstacles lurk in every nook and corner. Mikki's parents gave her a foolproof system to survive and thrive in such circumstances by making her brave and resilient. They empowered her to take difficulties in her stride, face them with composure and courage (not to mention the immense maturity that she cultivated in herself), and keep surging ahead despite the roadblocks that life may throw her way. They helped her assimilate the difference between bravery and brashness; that sometimes taking no action was better than taking a reckless action. They showed her the multifaceted face of bravery. It sometimes means speaking out or sometimes means remaining silent, it means being the bigger person and letting go but it also means fighting firmly for your rights. And the most important aspect that they taught her was understanding what bravery means in different situations.

The foundation of bravery is confidence. Especially for tender minds like Mikki's, they will get an internal 'go ahead!' for anything they want to express or oppose against only if they know there's a security blanket waiting for them in which they can curl up and hide against the piercing gaze of the outside world. And it's the parents who are tasked with holding up that security blanket and wrapping their child in its soft, warm, and safe folds. Mikki's parents, right from Day 1, instilled this confidence in her. They let her explore her surroundings to satisfy her curiosity, but always waited behind to catch her if she should stumble. When she would be shy to talk, they would convince her that her words held power and she should never be conscious of using it. If ever she had a fight with her friends and they were unfair to her, Mikki's first instinct was to withdraw into a cocoon and try to make peace of the situation. This is often a drawback of deeply kind and empathetic people (and Mikki has been established as that) because they think deeply on behalf of other people and don't want to hurt them in any way.

But Mikki's parents taught her a way to keep these beautiful traits of her character alive while also being fearless in confronting people. Mikki would, after putting up a brave face during the fight, run back home and lose herself in her mother's embrace. She would like to sit there while reaching out her hand to grasp her father's hand- this was the ultimate safe spot for her. She would then tearfully narrate the incident of the fight to them, and they would lovingly tell her that it was okay to call out a friend if the friend was doing something wrong. Mikki's biggest and utterly innocent worry, *"Will they stop talking to me if I do that?"* gradually vanished with her parents' reaffirmations that it was necessary to speak up against mean or unfair actions of others. Once these lessons planted themselves firmly in her mind, Mikki got the confidence to counter her friends, and over time, it extended to countering anyone who had it coming their way.

Her parents also continually nurtured her self-assurance that she could tell right from wrong. She created a set of core values and beliefs for herself based on what she saw around her, and her parents encouraged her to speak up against anything or anyone who went against this. Her values and beliefs, like a GPS, navigated her through various experiences, told her when to continue on the path that she was on and when a deviation was necessary. Mikki could then exhibit her bravery when the situations called for it, for she knew she always needed to be in places and be with the people who could help uphold and enrich her values and beliefs.

It is easy to remain positive and motivated when things are going our way. The real test of resilience, which goes hand in hand with bravery, is how positive or motivated one can remain in the face of adversity. Once the roots of resilience get planted in someone's mind, they quickly spread and grow, and help stabilize the person with their immense strength against harsh winds and storms. Mikki will, undoubtedly, face challenges as she grows up for it is the very essence of the thrilling journey called life that we have all embarked upon. The challenges may come from external sources and sometimes they stem from deep within. But resilience has the power to overcome any and all types of challenges. It is useful in every walk of life, be it personal or professional.

A personality like Mikki's, deeply imbibed with this trait, has a natural edge over the numerous others who are running in the race of life. Being bold and brave has a tendency to make the people who exhibit these traits a thorn in the side of others who do not. People do not appreciate being called out for their misdeeds. The ones who do the calling out hence often end up being ostracised and find themselves all alone despite having done nothing wrong. Resilience is what really matters in such situations; it alone has the power to tide a person through these unfavorable times and maintain their inner peace despite the crushing force of their external circumstances.

Mikki's parents used a special technique while trying to inculcate bravery and resilience in their daughter. They put up real examples and exceptional role models for her. Previously, if Mikki's mother found herself in a tough spot at office, she would discuss it with her husband and eventually decide to let it go. But after Mikki, and when their daughter was old and wise enough to understand their discussions, she made it a point to change her approach too and never settled for anything. She knew her daughter would mirror her actions, and she wanted Mikki to learn the right things.

Whenever Mikki's father would feel frustrated about having to travel so much for work, he would express it and rant it out, but he would always end it on a positive note that showed his daughter how to power through problems. Seeing them practically embodying the traits that they were trying to teach her made all the difference for Mikki. Additionally, her mother told her innumerable stories of goddesses, and Mikki too took an avid interest in them. With these fierce figures as her role models, Mikki had a strong vision of what she wanted to embody, and she achieved immense success in it.

Like with other values of kindness, compassion, and maturity, one person's bravery helps not just themselves but many others around them too. It entails standing up for oneself and others alike. Mikki learned from her parents to not let anyone ever take her for granted. Though it took time because of her inherently gentle and loving nature, she picked up the learning with time. However, from her own experiences and understanding of the concept, she realized that it could be used to help others too. She became a tiny little avenger and used her bravery for the benefit of others. If a classmate was too shy to speak to the teacher, or her friend was stuck in any problem, Mikki would swiftly rise up to the occasion and become their voice. Ready to get the matter in light, no matter how unpopular. Straight. Well intentioned.

Story 5: The Guardian Angel

Mikki always had a special bond with one of her teachers in school. On the first day after she met the teacher, she had gone home and declared to her parents, "My new teacher, Charu Ma'am, is a fairy. Just like in my fairy stories, she is sweet and kind and pretty. I like her so much!" Mikki's parents had been highly intrigued to meet this new person who had so charmed their daughter, for almost every day after school Mikki had something to share about her teacher, ranging from how pretty her clothes were to the fun activities that she planned for the class. When they finally got a chance to meet the teacher, it was quickly evident that the special bond had formed both ways. The teacher too seemed exceptionally fond of Mikki; as she spoke to her parents about how compassionate, helpful to students and sincere Mikki was in class, she beckoned Mikki toward her and affectionately stroked her head. Since the summer vacations were due to start and the darling duo of the teacher-student would be separated for a while, Mikki looked very upset. The teacher gave her a big hug and told her that she too would miss Mikki every day of the vacation. That brought a beaming smile to Mikki's face and it reflected in the face of the teacher too.

A while later, Mikki heard that the teacher was getting married. In her comprehension of things, she knew her mother and father were 'married' but she was too young to understand what it actually stood for. When she heard the news, however, she ran home and asked her mother what it meant to get married since she was very curious and concerned about what her favorite teacher was getting into. Mikki's mother replied, "It means that two people start staying together, become best friends, and support each other." Mikki's eyes went wide on hearing this explanation; she took some time to assimilate it and then she thrust her chin out determinedly. It was an adorable sight for a small child to look quite so fierce. She took this time to create a *'Charu Ma'am's Marriage Journal'*, which had pictures from magazines on wedding decorations, make-up, dresses, wedding card designs and ideas for photo shoots. Mikki used to work on the journal everyday, going through newspapers, magazines, pamphlets from boutiques which her mother visited and cut out the best of the best photos for Charu ma'am to put in the journal. When the schools finally opened, Mikki gave the journal to Charu Ma'am, and said "I made this for you! I hope it will help you in planning and organizing the marriage. I have added pages for you to select designs for your wedding dress, centrepieces, decoration. I have even added phone numbers of caterers, and DJ".

The teacher's fiancé happened to drop by one day as school was finishing. Like they often did, Mikki and her teacher were talking and laughing away together when he walked toward them with a pleasant expression. The teacher said to Mikki, "He is the one I am going to marry. I especially called him today since you had told me so many times that you wanted to meet him." The fiancé bent down and pulled out a large bar of chocolate that he had brought for Mikki.

At first, she became very shy to speak to him and extended a tentative hand to accept the gift. Then suddenly, as if she remembered the true reason why she had wanted this meeting, she summoned up all the courage in her little heart and said, "You have to take care of her. My mumma told me that marriage means the two people always support each other. I know Charu Ma'am will do it because she is the best at everything. But you also have to. We all love Charu Ma'am a lot so she should never feel alone or be sad."

Both the adults present there were too surprised to even react. Alternatively, they exchanged glances at one another and then at Mikki, who was standing with her brows knotted and her arms crossed, waiting for an answer. The innocence and fierce protectiveness that she displayed for her loved one were heartwarming. She had put it all on the line and spoken so openly in front of a stranger; it was the bravery coursing through her veins that made her take such a strong stand for her teacher's happiness. She wanted to play her part in ensuring her teacher remained happy and she went much out of her comfort zone to initiate such a frank discussion; it was the sign of a true brave heart. After a few seconds of stunned silence, the teacher giggled and gave Mikki a loving hug. The fiancé too went down on his knees in front of her with a warm smile and said, "I promise Ma'am! I will always take care of your teacher."

Mikki was delighted with the outcome she had brought about and happily tucked into the chocolate she had received. The adults looked adoringly at her, for the experience they had just had was as rare as it was endearing.

<u>Story 6: When Courage Conquered All</u>

Mikki's mother had a special arrangement worked out with her daughter right from her childhood days. Whenever Mikki's mother needed to visit her office for urgent client meetings, Mikki was told to not unnecessarily make calls to her and only call if "aliens happened to swing by for a day-spend" at that particular time. Mikki had loudly chuckled upon hearing this and through this simple and fun system, had understood to not disturb her mother when she was caught up in emergencies.

On one such day, Mikki's mother's phone kept incessantly buzzing with numerous phone calls. When a colleague finally brought her the phone out of concern for the number of calls she was receiving, she was shocked to see multiple missed calls from Mikki, a few more from Mikki's teacher, Charu Ma'am, and others from unknown numbers. A cold fear clutched her heart and she immediately called back her daughter. Mikki was crying profusely on the phone; despite her mother's repeated pleas, she told her nothing and insisted that her mother first speak with Charu Ma'am. Mikki's mother quickly called the teacher and was told that Mikki had beaten up some boys from her class. As a mother deeply aware of her daughter's level-headed, composed, and gentle personality, this news seemed unbelievable to Mikki's mother. She pleaded with the teacher to tell her the whole story.

The version told to Mikki's mother was such: A boy from Mikki's class had tried to give her a red rose. As is typical with boys groups in school, a few of his friends had chimed in and started teasing Mikki with the nickname 'Bhabhi'. That had angered Mikki to such an extent that she had beaten up the boys badly, so much so that one needed to be taken to the hospital. The parents were furious, and theirs were the other unknown numbers that had called Mikki's mother so many times.

Mikki's mother was still not convinced; she knew her daughter was well-equipped to defend herself, when necessary, but she also knew that her daughter would not react like this if the events had indeed been like the teacher had described. Mikki's mother had the utmost faith in their upbringing, and she knew her daughter would not resort to such extreme measures over trivial teasing. She rushed home to find, to her utmost relief, that Mikki had calmed down slightly. She calmly asked her daughter for the truth; it confirmed her suspicions and strengthened her belief in her daughter's sensibilities.

The actual version of events, perhaps unknown to the teacher, was such: After Mikki's division had been changed, she had found no friends in her new class. She mostly kept to herself and devoted all her focus to her studies. The boy in question had taken a fancy for her and had tried approaching her many times in the past. His friends had also joined in the teasing and it made Mikki very uncomfortable. After telling the it makes her uncomfortable many times, Mikki decided to simply ignore them and not entertain their antics. Since the boy was a popular figure in the class, many girls would pointedly criticize Mikki about how she was flashing attitude and being mean to him. Her immense mental strength and belief in her values made her withstand all these comments, and she did not let it bother her too much.

These events had eventually led up to that day, when the boy had come in front of her and thrust a rose at her. After maintaining her composure for so long, Mikki naturally started losing her cool. When the relentless harassment did not show any signs of stopping, Mikki's patience was pushed over the brim and she took a hard swing at the boy. She then turned to his friends and landed some well-deserved kicks and punches at them too.

When Mikki's parents heard the true story, they hugged their daughter and praised her for her immense bravery. The support from her parents made a small smile break out on Mikki's face; though she knew that the boys got exactly what they deserved, hearing her parents support her actions cemented the belief in her mind that she had done nothing wrong.

That belief kept her going through the tough times that awaited her at school. She became the sole talking point in her class, and none of the words being uttered were kind toward her. The students made rude and unkind remarks whenever she passed by, but she held her head up high and continued walking ahead. The school had decided not to take the incident any further, perhaps because they had learned the actual events that had unfolded. Her mother ensured that the school knew that they stood by her, and did not condone bullying of any kind.

However, that did not stop the parents of the boys from calling Mikki's mother to complain and question her actions. Again, Mikki's mother made it a point to answer these calls in front of her daughter; she fiercely defended Mikki's actions and vehemently declared that she was proud of her, while criticizing the parents for the poor upbringing of their sons. Mikki's father went a step ahead and even taught her new punches and kicks; they practiced loudly and enthusiastically every evening!

In the end, Mikki understood one thing, boundaries are to be shown, not spoken. Some people will respect those boundaries, many will not, and she has to embrace this. The smart thing for her would be to be with people who appreciate and respect her sense of self, even if they are not the 'popular' ones in school or in any other sphere of her life.

Chapter Five: Community Cuddling Cub

"I need to look out for my interests."

"If it does not help me in any way, why should I do it?"

We hear these statements either being voiced out loud, or can discern them being mentally stated out in the actions of others. Doing things selflessly for the benefit of others, or working with the belief that the benefits of good actions should extend beyond oneself is fast disappearing amongst the shadows cast by selfishness and indifference.

But, amongst this, like a radiating light that casts a bright glow on everything and everyone that it touches, there comes the undying spirit of giving. And with this spirit comes Mikki, a small but sincere personification of this value.

Mikki's parents believed that the world is a reflection of one's thoughts. Everyone is innately good and wants to do their best. They tried to equip their daughter with the powerful virtue of generosity. They wanted her to experience the profound joy that comes from giving. They didn't teach Mikki about generosity through instructions or lessons, but through their own actions and the giving environment they created at home.

From a young age, Mikki saw her parents engage in acts of kindness and generosity daily. Mikki's mother often made extra mithai to share with guards, gardeners, and helpers, while her father never missed a chance to help the old lady at the grocery shop with her computer-related problems. Whenever Mikki's mother took Mikki along to give the mithaai, she explained that sharing multiplies the joys. Her father, on the other hand, showed Mikki the importance of lending a helping hand, not for recognition, but because it was the right thing to do. Mikki saw these acts of kindness, and soon enough, the concept became a deeply ingrained part of her personality.

She began actively participating in them, and they eventually started coming naturally to her. Mikki's parents involved her in community service activities, such as volunteering at local dog shelters or serving 'langar'. Mikki was brought up believing that 'seva' (serving others) is a way to earn blessings, and be grateful to the Almighty. These activities became family traditions that Mikki looked forward to, understanding that 'seva' was a way of life and not just an occasional act.

Mikki's parents also incorporated stories into their bedtime routine, stories of heroes who changed the world with their generosity. These stories were not just about famous people, but also about ordinary individuals whose small acts of kindness had a big impact. It was almost always that Mikki's soul absorbed the lesson and she consciously looked for opportunities to be kind to the world around her.

They wanted Mikki to understand that everyone makes a mark on themselves and others by making a choice on how to be, and could make a difference. The stories became a cherished getaway for Mikki, where she could lose herself in the beautiful world erected by generosity and selflessness, and where the seeds of the spirit of 'seva' were planted in her young heart.

Mikki, with her curious eyes and tender heart, absorbed these lessons eagerly and tried to replicate whatever good acts she did with her parents on her own. She saw giving as a way to make the world brighter and happier. When she saw her parents smile at the joy their small acts of kindness brought to others, Mikki felt a warm glow inside her. She started to find her own ways to give, in the pure and innocent manner that only a child can.

She would share her toys, even her most favorite stuffed teddy bear or the shoeboxes that she loved collecting with her friends when she saw how bothered they got over not having them. And the best part? She never did this because her parents forced her, but because she thought it was worth it if that simple act could make her friends happy. Right after she learned how to hold a crayon and write letters, she would rush to make cards for every birthday or festival, after learning that personal efforts go a long way. She even began to understand the value of giving her time, whether it was helping her mom in the kitchen or listening to her grandfather's stories that he longed to tell her, sometimes even when she got very bored of them! But she never let it show and amusedly kept listening to her beloved grandfather.

Mikki found joy in these moments, feeling connected to the people around her and realizing that giving was a way of building bridges and creating bonds.

As she grew older, her understanding of giving deepened. She realized that giving wasn't always about things; sometimes, all it took was offering a shoulder to cry on or a listening ear. Mikki learned to be there for her friends and family, offering support and comfort in times of need. And, of course, her immense kindness and bravery too created a fierce desire in her to look out for others and be protective. She understood that her presence and empathy were valuable gifts she could offer; she had nothing to lose by offering them but she and others had a lot to gain from it. This understanding made Mikki a true friend, a supportive family member, and a valuable member of society.

The spirit of 'seva' is a cornerstone of a compassionate society. When people like Mikki embrace this value and make it a part of their beliefs, they contribute to a world that is kinder and more inclusive. For Mikki, 'seva' helped her look beyond the shiny glare of grand gestures, which she as a child did not have the means to do, and realize that small and thoughtful gestures have much more power. If more people uncovered this power and made the spirit of giving their way of life, the world would be brimming with happiness and empathy.

Giving also promotes a sense of belonging and purpose. When people give, they often feel more connected to their people and more invested in the well-being of others. It makes one realize that as young or uninfluential as they may be, nothing can stop them from making a difference in someone's life if they really want to. It makes one feel like they are part of something much bigger than themselves and most beautiful too.

Moreover, the spirit of 'seva' can have an enormous positive impact on the well-being of the giver and receiver, which makes every person the best version of themselves. For Mikki, this meant experiencing the joy and satisfaction that came from making a good contribution to someone's life. It taught her that "seva" can have a domino effect. She learned that one act of 'seva' spells a powerful narrative for others. By experiencing 'seva' they know that they are not alone; that someone is there to help them, look out for them, and be their guiding light along challenging and difficult paths. The world would be a much more joyous place if everyone could experience such well-being.

The spirit of 'seva' also encourages a culture of gratitude. When people give and receive generously, they start to appreciate the kindness and support they get from others. This makes them feel happier and stronger. For Mikki, learning to value the kindness of others helped her develop a positive attitude and a deep sense of thankfulness for everything in her life.

Story 7: Cleanliness is Next to Godliness

From a young age, Mikki was fascinated by the stories of goddesses, especially Goddess Saraswati, who blessed us with knowledge and wisdom. Her mother often shared stories about Saraswati, explaining that all things related to learning and knowledge should be treated with the utmost respect. "Goddess Saraswati resides in your books and papers," her mother would say. "We must treat them with care and never let them touch the ground."

On one afternoon, Mikki's mother took her to the local market. As they moved through the crowded streets, Mikki suddenly stopped. She stared intently at something and her eyes teared up. Her lower lip started quivering, and her usually cheerful face looked immensely sad.

Concerned, her mother instantly knelt down beside her. "What is it, Mikki?" she asked gently.

Mikki pointed to a piece of paper lying on the ground. "Mumma, it's paper," she said, her voice trembling. "We shouldn't let it be dirty. Goddess Saraswati won't like it. She will get angry with everyone here."

Her mother watched in awe as Mikki picked up the litter with her tiny hands, brushed off the dirt, and said softly, "Sorry, Goddess Saraswati. From all of us." She then ran to the nearest bin and threw the paper away.

Seeing her daughter's earnestness in keeping the community clean and pleasing Goddess Saraswati for the benefit of all, Mikki's mother couldn't help but smile with pride.

"You're right, Mikki. Let's show respect to Goddess Saraswati," she said. That evening, the two of them spent hours in the market, picking up littered paper. As she got tucked into bed that night, Mikki delightedly told her mother, "I feel so happy that we cleaned up the market for everyone!"

When the Swachh Bharat Abhiyan campaign was launched by the Indian Prime Minister, the message of cleanliness resonated deeply with Mikki. She was older now, but her respect for cleanliness in the community had only grown stronger. Mikki was moved by the idea of contributing to a cleaner India and decided to take action in her own neighborhood. One Saturday morning, Mikki gathered her friends and said, "Let's help clean our community," she said with excitement in her eyes. "We can make a difference just like the Prime Minister said!"

And she had it all planned out too. "We'll clean the park today. I talked to the cleaning lady at home, and she taught me about wet and dry waste. We can do this!" she elatedly told her friends.

They spent their weekend picking up litter, sorting it into wet and dry waste bins, and encouraging others to join them. Mikki's enthusiasm was contagious. "Did you know," she told her friends, "If we keep our streets clean, we're showing respect not just to our community but to ourselves too!"

Mikki's action plan was not limited to the park. At home too, she became a vigilant guardian of cleanliness. She made sure the garbage was correctly segregated and often stood by the kitchen bin to check if the waste was properly sorted. She emphatically told her family how much easier it would be for the cleaning lady and for garbage recycling if they all made small changes at home.

Her words swayed them all, and small as she was, she played a big part in making a healthier, prettier, and more considerate community. And it all started with a little girl who believed in the magic of respecting knowledge and the importance of keeping her surroundings clean.

Story 8: Children for Children

As Mikki grew older, her desire to help people and the ways in which she could do this increased. This spirit of giving, nurtured by her parents from a young age, manifested in various ways throughout her life. One such way was her creation of the YouTube channel, "Children for Children."

Mikki was always a keen observer of the world around her. She noticed that many of her peers and friends were dealing with real challenges like bullying, feeling isolated when schools shifted online during the pandemic, and being afraid of public speaking. Her maturity gave her a new lens to look at this problem with; she realized that if almost all the children she knew were facing some or the other difficulties, it must be such a widespread problem. She never felt or claimed that she could solve it, but she simply thought of bringing everyone together to share experiences or suggestions, so that they could collectively find a way around their difficulties.

She knew that adults often provided advice on these topics, but she believed that hearing from fellow children could make a significant impact. She wanted her friends and other children to know that they were not alone in their struggles. Mikki wanted to simply give everyone a safe spot to openly discuss their challenges and learn from each other's experiences.

The idea for "Children for Children" was born out of this desire to help. Mikki approached a few friends with her idea, and they were immediately on board. Together, they planned and produced three episodes, each focusing on a different topic. The goal was to address the issues that most children faced and provide practical advice from a child's perspective.

In the first episode, they tackled stage fright. Mikki knew from her own experience that performing in front of others could be terrifying. She invited her friend, who was an excellent public speaker, to share tips on overcoming nervousness and building confidence. Mikki hoped that by hearing from someone else their age, the other listeners of her channel would feel encouraged to face their fears. The second episode focused on dealing with bullying. This was a topic close to Mikki's heart, as she had seen friends suffer from bullying and wanted to help. She brought in another friend who had successfully stood up to bullies and created a safe environment for herself at school. The friend shared her story and provided practical advice on how to handle bullies, encouraging children to speak up and seek help when needed. In the third episode, they discussed maintaining friendships during online schooling. Mikki and her friends shared their own experiences of staying in touch with friends through video calls, online games, and other creative ways. They wanted to reassure others that it was possible to maintain strong friendships even without meeting or being together.

Mikki also wanted to ensure that the discussions did not remain limited to kiddy discussions, however important she believed those to be. She invited one of the friends' mother's to join each episode. They shared a parent's viewpoint on the issues discussed, bridging the gap between children and adults. The insights were valuable in helping children understand how their parents saw these problems and what they could do to support their kids.

Mikki put in her life and soul into thinking about every small detail of her channel, and how she could make it more meaningful. She spent hours thinking from the shoes of her friends, wondering what they would like to hear or what measures she could take to help them.

They were driven by the belief that their efforts could make a difference in the lives of other children. The joy of giving back and helping others was her primary motivation and she found delight whenever she could make even a slight difference to someone's life. Unfortunately, despite her enthusiasm and hard work, the channel did not gain the popularity they had hoped for. After three episodes, she decided to take a break. However, Mikki didn't view this as a failure. She was proud of what she had accomplished and the positive feedback she had received from those who watched the episodes. Whenever she thought back about it, Mikki realized that the spirit of giving wasn't about the number of views or subscribers.

It was about the effort to make a difference, no matter how small. She had created a platform that allowed children to voice their concerns and support each other, even if it was only for a short while. The experience taught her valuable lessons in empathy, collaboration, and the impact of community support. She learnt that social platforms are a strong channel to join voices and get heard. The channel may no longer be active, but the essence of what she aimed to achieve continues to inspire her. Mikki learned that the act of giving comes in many forms, and sometimes, the most meaningful contributions are those that come from the heart, without expecting anything in return. Her story is a reminder that the spirit of giving is not measured by the scale of the gesture, but by the intention and love behind it. Mikki's journey is a beautiful example of how a young girl, driven by empathy and a desire to help, can make a significant difference in the world around her.

Chapter Six: Firm But Gentle

For her parents, Mikki was and would always remain special. Not only because she was their daughter, but she came to them at a point when they were at the lowest of their lows. She made some of the toughest days feel like a walk in the breeze. They sometimes dearly wished they could always keep her nestled within their hearts, where she would be safe from the pressures and demands of the cutthroat world. They wished they could do something which would make Mikki never have to worry about anything, fight for her rights in the face of difficulties, or have to bear any kind of tension. But, like every hopeful parent desiring this for their child, they realized it could not be done. Instead, they focussed on what could be done. How Mikki could have a strong moral compass that equipped her to deal with tricky or sensitive situations that came her way, and how she could be set up for success and happiness in whatever she chose to do.

How she could be taught discipline.

Realizing its immense importance early on, Mikki's parents made discipline a cornerstone in her upbringing. Her parents appreciated the highly significant role it played in shaping her approach to life.

They believed that teaching Mikki discipline early on would help her build productive habits, a strong work ethic, and a sense of personal accountability, which would benefit her throughout life. Most importantly, they wanted her to learn that discipline means having self-control and making the right choices, even when it was hard.

As in all their other important lessons for their daughter, Mikki's parents did not choose the path of instilling discipline in her through strict rules. They realized the slight but important difference between making Mikki follow a disciplined life because they were telling her to do so, as opposed to nudging her toward choosing a life of discipline for herself and making her see the benefits in it. They gently guided her toward understanding the essence of this value through everyday routines and consistent behavior. When she was a small child, the complex term 'discipline' could not be understood by her, but the behavior that she saw around her could well be understood and imitated. Mikki's parents wanted her to see discipline as a ladder that would help her achieve her dreams; it would take many small and sincere steps to get her where she wanted to be. They made her see it as a means rather than an end.

Mikki had a structured day, starting with a consistent wake-up time. Every morning, she would lovingly wake up Mikki at a specific time, that was differently planned for school times and vacation times (again, in the spirit of not making Mikki feel burdened by routines). For the first few years of her life, Mikki's mother had to specifically teach Mikki to brush her teeth, make her bed, and drink her milk. As this order of things started feeling comfortable and welcoming to Mikki, she started doing it on her own. Mikki's mother knew she had imparted an early lesson in discipline that would help her daughter till much later in life.

Mikki's father, on the other hand, focused on goal-setting and sincerely carrying them through. There was a storybook that Mikki adored, and she was excited to attempt reading it after she had learned reading in school. On the first day, when it seemed too difficult, she looked dejected and almost gave up. That's when her father taught her that real discipline means "one step forward everyday" toward something that you wish to achieve. Mikki tried that, and she would sit with the book and try to read one page daily. Even if she got back late after playing with her friends, or was tired from schoolwork, she never missed a day of reading. At the end of a month, when she happily read the book out to her parents, her father was delighted at how she had tackled the challenge in front of her.

"FDTD. First Deserve, Then Desire"- Through their own actions too, Mikki's parents demonstrated how discipline could become a part of their daily lives. Her mother always finished her work before relaxing, showing Mikki that leisure time was a reward for hard work. Her father made it a point to exercise regularly, however tired he was, teaching Mikki the importance of sticking to the commitments that one makes to themselves and to others. They led by example, showing Mikki that discipline was a part of every aspect of life, from schoolwork to hobbies, to personal care.

As Mikki grew up, she began to see discipline as a tool that helped her achieve what she wanted. To her, discipline wasn't just about following rules made by someone else. She realized that she had to make and follow the rules for herself and those rules would benefit her in whatever she did.

Mikki understood that discipline helped her in her schoolwork. By setting aside time each day to do her homework, she found that she could understand her lessons better and keep up with her classmates. She started to enjoy the feeling of being prepared for her classes and the sense of accomplishment that came with completing her assignments on time. She also saw the perks of discipline in her hobbies. Like her father had taught her for reading (which she went on to practice for every other book too that she wanted to read), she got better at almost every activity like sports, painting, drawing, etc. simply by being disciplined about practising it. This small, consistent effort made a big difference, and Mikki felt proud of her progress.

She also embraced discipline in her daily routines. At first, she would do a particular chore on one day and then forget to do it the next few days. Mikki's mother too never pushed her to do it, for she knew her daughter would eventually understand. Mikki then realized that it was only through discipline that she could truly contribute to the house and help her parents. After learning this important lesson, she started helping her mother with chores around the house, understanding that these tasks were necessary to keep their home neat and tidy. Day after day, these tasks became a part of her life. She would set the table before dinner, tidy up her room every evening, and help with the dishes. These small acts of discipline went on to become habits and made her feel responsible and helpful.

Mikki's parents continued to nurture her sense of discipline with gentle guidance and encouragement. They praised her for her consistent efforts and discussed the importance of staying committed to her goals. They explained that discipline wasn't about being perfect, but about trying your best and hardest, and not giving up.

But most importantly, Mikki's parents taught her about the importance of balance. They explained that while discipline was crucial, it was also essential to take breaks and have fun. Discipline could very easily slip into rigidity, and they did not want their daughter to become rigid with her routines, for it was the unhealthiest form of discipline. They showed her that sometimes, simply taking a break from everything and not doing daily tasks was equally important. What mattered was that she got back to those tasks after a well-deserved break. And through these teachings, Mikki learned that discipline was not about being strict or rigid but about being consistent and making wise choices. She realized that discipline was a form of self-love, helping her to take care of herself and achieve her dreams.

Discipline is the pillar on which high stacks of growth and development can stand. For individuals like Mikki, learning to be disciplined means developing the ability to set goals and work towards them with determination and perseverance. It helps build resilience, allowing her to overcome obstacles and stay focused on her path. In the broader context, discipline creates a sense of responsibility and integrity in a person. When people are disciplined, they are more likely to fulfill their commitments since they will keep working sincerely toward them. It also encourages productivity and efficiency. When individuals manage their time well and stay organized, they can accomplish more and make significant contributions in their professional and personal lives.

One of the most important aspects of discipline that Mikki learned was the value of self-control. She understood that sometimes she had to say no to some things that sounded like fun to achieve things that were not as fun, but which would help her much more. These choices (which seemed difficult at the moment) eventually helped her develop self-discipline and taught her the importance of prioritizing her responsibilities. By setting goals and working towards them, she felt empowered and confident. Her parents encouraged her to set her own routines, and she felt in charge.

As a young girl, she would sit with multiple papers and colored pencils around her to try to create nice timetables for herself- when to study, when to play, when to spend time with her parents, etc. The amount of thought and effort she put into it was amusing and heartwarming to see; her parents smiled upon seeing her scribble vigorously to plan the routines and watched with delight as she struck off whatever she had achieved in the day every night before going to bed; their daughter had learned the lessons of discipline that they wanted to impart to her and had embraced them in her own innocent way.

Story 9: Should Discipline be Limited to Oneself?

Mikki's inherent discipline not only shaped her own life but also inspired those around her to adopt healthier habits. This was most evident in her mission to make her father and his close friends (all of whom she affectionately called "Chachu") quit smoking. Mikki, the first baby in her father's immediate circle of school friends, was loved and pampered by all of them. Whenever she attended their late-night parties with her parents, the "Chachus", made sure to organize Maggi and keep Disney movies ready, ensuring that she too would have the best time there. Her presence at these gatherings and her curious nature led to her seeing the adults smoking one night. Her young mind absorbed the information, but she did not know what to do with it.

One day, after watching an anti-smoking advertisement in a movie theater, Mikki's mind made a very disturbing connection. The ad showed the severe health consequences of smoking, and Mikki, with her disciplined mind and caring heart, couldn't ignore it.

With tears in her eyes and tension etched into her face, she turned to her father and asked, "Did you know that smoking is dangerous, Papa? Do Chachus know this?"

Her father, at a complete loss for words, admitted that they were aware of the dangers but assured her that they didn't smoke often. This answer didn't satisfy Mikki. She began to cry loudly and asked, "If you know it is wrong and dangerous, why are you all still doing it? You told me not to climb on that high tree because I could get hurt. I loved doing it but still, I stopped. Why can't you stop?"

Her question hit the target, and her father realized that it was a test of the discipline that he had worked hard to pass on to his daughter. When they returned home, Mikki insisted that her father call each of her Chachus so she could talk to them. She explained the ad that she had seen which told her how dangerous smoking was and how much she cared for them. She then revisited the story of her and the tree climbing and insisted that her father and Chachus too to give up something that they liked because it was bad for them; little as she was, she had unknowingly challenged them to prove their self-discipline and match the level of discipline that she had exhibited.

However, old habits die hard, and they could not quit immediately. They became cleverer, hiding their cigarettes and lighters whenever Mikki was around, using mouth spray before greeting her, and going to great lengths to conceal their smoking. Despite their numerous tactics, Mikki's determination to ensure they all were disciplined never lessened. She would routinely check on them, and if she detected any signs of smoking, she didn't hesitate to call them out for it (the mature and brave girl that she is!) How many packs of cigarettes Nattu Chachu had to hide, is no joke!

In this way, Mikki's discipline not only shaped her own character but also positively influenced those she loved. Her story is a beautiful example of how the values instilled in a young girl can lead to meaningful change in the lives of others. Through her disciplined efforts, Mikki demonstrated that true discipline goes beyond personal habits; it's about caring for others and helping them become better versions of themselves.

Story 10: Eat, Sleep, Practise, Repeat

On one sunny afternoon, Mikki requested her mother to accompany her to the basketball court. Her mother readily agreed, thinking it would simply be a fun afternoon wherein she could watch her daughter play; instead, it turned out to be a long and impactful lesson in discipline that left her inspired.

Mikki had her sights on an unshakeable goal- she wanted to get 300 shots into the hoop. She started with a series of warm-up shots, aiming carefully, and focusing on the form that was taught to her. For every successful shot, there were several misses, but Mikki didn't let that shake her resolve. With each missed shot, she would pause, think about what could have gone wrong, and try again. Mikki's mother watched in awe as she missed almost 200 shots, but she kept pushing and grinding till she completed her set target of getting 300 shots right.

Mikki's mother could not help but feel the utmost pride in her daughter's resilience and commitment to the game Mikki loved. From that day onwards, her daughter became a role model in discipline and perseverance for her; and what happier feeling could there be for a parent than having their child become their role model?! Mikki's mother watched in amazement as her daughter, without letting the disappointment of failure bring her down or without making any excuses for herself, picked up the ball each time and kept shooting it tirelessly. She thought to herself, "If this little one is so committed and is not giving up, why do we adults not make the same efforts for our goals?". She understood that there can be many excuses to say No, but there is only one reason to Yes. That is the love for the thing you want to do.

Mikki had not intended for this intense practice session to simply last for one day- she had bigger plans for herself. She wanted her technique to be deeply refined and wanted to keep practicing and become brilliant in the basics. Mikki's mother often joined her at practice, not just to offer support but also to witness Mikki's growth and determination. She would sit on the sidelines, cheering for every successful shot and offering words of encouragement when Mikki's frustration began to show. Despite the occasional tears, rants of frustration, and moments of doubt, Mikki never gave up. For several weeks, this routine became Mikki's life. She would come home from school, quickly finish her homework, and then head to the court. There was no time for distractions or other activities; her focus was solely on basketball. Each day, she grew a little stronger, a little more skilled, and a lot more confident.

She became a wonderful example of how discipline paved the path for personal growth and achievements.

One person's discipline has the power to inspire many others to keep working toward their own goals without stopping, tiring, or giving up. And if the person embodying such values is an adorable young girl with a wonderful mindset, who would not want to follow suit?

Chapter Seven: Grateful Hearts; Humble Souls

"A grateful heart is a beginning of greatness. It is an expression of humility."

- James Faust

-

The importance of the values of gratitude and humility is beautifully captured in this quote.

Gratitude is the key that opens doors to a happier and more content life. Without being mindful and thankful of the things that one has been blessed with in life, they will always be stuck in a rut of wanting more and more. Instead, gratitude makes one see everything that they already have and find happiness within those. Humility, on the other hand, is the crowning glory of a person's character. Without it, one can often get caught up in limiting emotions like pride and selfishness, which do not make for welcome additions in one's personality. Humility is the stabilizing force in one's life, which keeps them grounded and in touch with their roots.

Teaching children these values, and seeing how it shapes their innocent minds to impact their actions is a wonderful journey; one that Mikki's parents embarked upon very early in her life and to date, find thoroughly enjoyable and rewarding.

Such complex, nuanced, and significant values are difficult for a child to even imagine, leave alone understand and implement. However, that's where parents come in. They play a crucial role in making these concepts simple for children, through everyday actions and conversations. By expressing thankfulness for both big and small blessings, parents can show their children how to appreciate what they have. They can also teach humility by showing respect for others, regardless of their status or material possessions, or by admitting to their own mistakes and showing a willingness to learn and grow.

Mikki's parents knew that teaching their daughter to be grateful and humble was one of the greatest gifts they could give her. It would be the blueprint to mould her into a person loved and respected by all, and it would also be instrumental in ensuring that she loved and respected herself too, while remaining down-to-earth. And hence, in Mikki's home, gratitude and humility were gently blended into the fabric of their lives and without realizing it, Mikki was quickly embraced in their warm hold.

Her parents showed gratitude by thanking each other for small acts of kindness, like making a cup of tea or helping with chores. They also made a habit of expressing thanks for things like the food on their table, the roof over their heads, and the love they shared as a family. Mikki absorbed these lessons, learning to say "thank you" often and to genuinely appreciate all the things she had in life.

Humility too echoed in Mikki's home, and made its occupants nice and kind human beings. Her parents taught her to be respectful and kind to everyone, no matter who they were. Mikki knew very well that 'Didi' at home was not there to serve her, but to help her mother in running the house smoothly. Mikki was encouraged to do her own work- as small as keeping her washed clothes in her almirah, to serving guests when her parents hosted parties. They showed her that everyone has something valuable to offer and that it's important to listen and learn from others. They also demonstrated humility by admitting when they were wrong and apologizing sincerely, showing Mikki that it's okay to make mistakes and that the true strength lies in acknowledging them and making amends.

Mikki, with her curious mind and tender heart, understood these values in her own special way. She took the lessons, and gave it a unique spin by blending her own innocence, compassion, maturity, bravery, discipline, and all the other wonderful traits she possessed; and it sure became something magical and extraordinary. She began to show gratitude by thanking her friends and teachers, not just for gifts or help, but also for their friendship, kindness, and patience whenever an opportunity came. She would write little notes or draw pictures to express her thanks, often surprising her loved ones with her heartfelt gestures. Because she felt that when gifts are personalised, they become more special.

In school, Mikki started to stand out as a humble and kind student. She never boasted about her achievements (and her hard work led to her having quite many feathers in her cap), and instead, always gave credit where she believed it was due- either to her parents for all the help they gave her, or to her teachers for giving her the right knowledge and wisdom. She always tried to help her classmates, whether it was with schoolwork or just being there to listen. Mikki's humility made her approachable and well-loved among her peers. She treated everyone with the same respect, whether it was the janitor or the principal, and she always had a kind word or a smile for everyone she met.

The importance of these values is profound, especially for children. Gratitude helps children develop a positive outlook on life. When they learn to appreciate what they have, they are more likely to find joy in everyday moments and retain the blissful innocence, free from materialistic expectations, that is one of the most cherished characteristics of childhood. This positive attitude can lead to greater happiness and resilience, helping them to cope better with challenges and setbacks. Humility, on the other hand, teaches children to value others and to understand that everyone has their own strengths and weaknesses. It helps them build better relationships based on mutual respect and kindness. Humble children are more likely to be empathetic, understanding, and supportive, making them good friends and valued members of their community.

For Mikki, these values became a natural part of who she was. She learned that being thankful and humble made her feel more connected to the people around her. She realized that her words and actions could bring joy to others, and this, in turn, made her happy. Mikki's journey in understanding and practicing gratitude and humility not only enriched her life but also brought light and love to those around her.

Even as a child, Mikki's journey of embracing these values was a joyous and fulfilling ride and it only became better with time. As her world expanded, she met new people and gained new experiences, and her thinking evolved, her understanding of these values deepened and she began doing more amazing things with them. She realized that simply saying 'thank you' for the sake of it versus feeling it deep within her heart were two very different scenarios, and they made her think very differently about everything around her. The values had to come inherently to her, and become a part of her core personality.

As she grew older, Mikki's understanding of these values deepened. She saw that gratitude wasn't just about saying thank you; it was about feeling it in her heart and showing it through her actions. She learned to be grateful not only for the good times but also for the challenges that taught her valuable lessons. This deeper sense of gratitude made her more resilient and optimistic. Similarly, Mikki's humility grew stronger with time. She understood that being humble didn't mean thinking less of herself, but rather thinking about herself lesser. She learned to celebrate others' successes without feeling envious and to accept praise with grace. Mikki's humility allowed her to form deeper, more meaningful connections with people, as they felt seen and valued by her.

These values shine brightly as guiding stars along the path of Mikki's life. Her parents' loving example and her own pure-hearted efforts made these values an integral part of her character. Mikki is the small yet solid proof of the power of these simple and significant values, showing us all that a grateful heart and a humble spirit can create bursts of joy and kindness in the world.

And so, the heartwarming story she is building, in which gratitude and humility serve as main characters, continues. These values, instilled in her from a young age, continue to guide her as she navigates the world. They help her to see the beauty in everyday moments and to find joy in helping others. Mikki's journey reminds us all of the importance of being thankful for our blessings and of treating everyone with kindness and respect. Through her simple, innocent acts, Mikki shows us that even the smallest person can make a big difference in the world, one thankful and humble step at a time.

Story 11: The Beacon of Humility

Mikki was a child who always stood out. Her teachers in the first and second grades nicknamed her "Sunshine Smile" because of her cheerful and happy demeanor that touched others too and spread much like warm and mellow sunshine. It was the most apt nickname!

She excelled in extracurricular activities and was always the first choice for school functions, inter-school competitions, and even state and national level events. She was a state-level winner in under-10 and under-12 skating, a national gold medalist in yoga, a silver medalist in track, and a winner of numerous school awards for best dancer, best debater, and best in theater.

But despite all her wonderful achievements, Mikki remained truly humble. One day, during a parent-teacher meeting, her teacher remarked, "Mikki, why don't you put this effort into math and science too? If you do, you could be the topper and win the trophy of the Best Student."

Mikki replied with a gentle smile, "Ma'am, I put a lot of effort into these other activities because I know I'm not good at math and science. My low grades in these subjects hurt me a lot, especially when my friends are class and subject toppers. But I know I have to accept that I cannot be good at everything. Why should I spend my time and effort on something I know I can't do as well? I don't have to top the class, and I feel so happy to leave winning the best student award to my friends."

Her teacher was taken aback by her honesty and maturity. Mikki's mother, who was also present, felt a swell of pride. Mikki wasn't boastful about her accomplishments; she stayed grounded, never letting her successes go to her head or come between her and her friends.

One time, Mikki and her mother visited one of her friend's house. The friend's daughter talked endlessly about her awards and achievements, including being a winner of the World Scholars Cup for her school. That night, as they were heading home, Mikki's mother quietly asked, "Mikki, you have more accomplishments than you can possibly talk about. Why did you stay silent and not share them at all?"

Mikki, in her usual calm and innocent manner, replied, "Because I don't sit with it, Mumma. When I win something, I enjoy the attention from everyone that day, and then I'm okay the next day. I work towards the next competition. I'm happy for Arushi (that was the name of the boastful little girl). I hope she does well with the World Scholars Cup."

Mikki's mother was silent for a moment, then smiled. She had learned a valuable lesson from her daughter: humility also means giving space to others to enjoy their time in the spotlight. It means not overshadowing others with your own successes. Mikki's wisdom echoed in her mind and like many times before, gave her a new perspective through which to see the world.

Mikki's ability to stay grounded despite her numerous achievements was remarkable. She never let her wins get to her head. Instead, she focused on the joy of the journey and the friendships she cherished. Her mother marveled at how Mikki's humility shone brightly, making her a beloved star among her peers.

One day, while they were sitting in the garden, Mikki's mother asked her, "How do you manage to stay so humble? I've never even heard you ask me or Papa for a simple gift for all the things you have achieved!"

Mikki looked up at the sky and said, "I don't think I need gifts for anything that I've done. And besides, you both keep doing things for me even without me asking! And I don't like talking much about my achievements because I don't want anyone to feel bad; I realize not everyone is as lucky as me to get the opportunities that I do. Nobody should ever feel bad because of me."

Her mother nodded, feeling grateful for her wise little girl. Mikki's approach to life was simple yet profound. She understood that true success was not just about winning awards but also about being kind, humble, and supportive of others.

Story 12: The Glow of Gratitude

Mikki's parents believed that gratitude meant being content with what you have. They taught her that while it was one thing to aim for more luxurious items, they emphasized that not having them did not lessen one's worth as a person.

In the school environment, parents often miss the subtleties of their children's social circles. They don't always know the contents of each lunch box, who owns the latest school bag, who sports a Garmin watch, or who uses the newest iPhone to make reels in the washroom. Despite believing they understand their children's world, they only catch glimpses through birthday parties, school functions, and Parent-Teacher Meetings. It was the same for Mikki's parents too.

One such meeting marked the beginning of a new school session. Mikki had excelled in the previous term, earning awards and good grades, and her parents were delighted with her performance.

They promised to get her the school supplies of her choice. They suggested she go for the colorful and trendy set from a popular brand, Smiggles. Excited, Mikki made a sweet list of all the school supplies she wanted, including her favorite stores like Chumbak and

The Drama Queen. They even encouraged her to add clothes for an upcoming birthday party. The three of them eagerly planned a day at the mall, filled with excitement.

When they arrived at the mall and stood outside the store, they asked Mikki for her list. She handed it over, and to their immense surprise, they saw that next to many items she had written notes like, "I have," "Not needed," "Have an alternative," and "Can see." Her parents exchanged puzzled looks.

"What is this, Mikki?" her mother asked, genuinely astonished at the list.

Mikki smiled and said, "I thought about it later, and I really don't need anything. I already have what I need. My Natraj eraser erases just as well as the Smiggles one would. The same goes for the sharpener and colored pencils. Buying new ones doesn't make sense to me."

They reminded her of the Kipling bag she had admired her friend carrying during the last Parent-Teacher Meeting.

"Should we get you that?" they enthusiastically asked in unison.

"I had liked it, but it does the same thing my bag does! If you want to buy me something, please buy me new tassels to put on my bag! It will make it look so colorful."

Mikki's parents looked at each other, both thinking the same thing- How pure were the thoughts of their daughter that as opposed to all the extravagant things they wanted to indulge her with, she instead found happiness in a handful of tassels?! They were amazed at her clarity and lack of greed. She was content with what she had. Mikki's mother felt a deep sense of pride. "You're right, Mikki. And it's wonderful that you know what you need and what you don't."

Mikki nodded and then innocently said, "I just want a nice shirt for the birthday party. Can I get that?" Her parents happily obliged.

They also decided to get her a new bag since her old one was tearing at the side. When her parents reminded her of the same and her mind quickly made the distinction between it being a 'need' instead of a 'want', it was like her conscience eased up about the purchase and she excitedly took her time to select a new bag.

That evening, as they returned home, her parents hugged her tightly. "Mikki, you're a wonderful girl. We're so proud of you."

She beamed at them and said, "Even if I've got many hugs from you both before, I always need more and more of those!"

They chuckled at her sweet humor, and soaked in her brightness that radiated over everyone and everything.

Her mindset was a beautiful reminder that gratitude can indeed make life richer and more fulfilling.

Chapter Eight: The Fragile Bridges of Friendship

Life is like a bumpy ride, always filled with twists and turns. Some of these turns will take us to happy places, but some of them come in a more difficult form that challenges us and everything we stand for.

Teaching children how to go ahead on this road without getting blindsided by the challenges and tripping over the obstacles is one of the most important lessons parents can impart. Just like the sun shines brightest after a scary storm, children shine with an inherent glow of confidence and courage when they overcome challenges. Helping children cope with difficulties hands them the most useful GPS they will need to navigate life's bumpy ride.

At home, Mikki's parents believed in talking openly about challenges and made it a regular practice. They encouraged her to express her feelings and to ask for help when she needed it. And they led by example too, by themselves asking each other or even her for help whenever the need came. They taught her that it's okay to make mistakes and that the solution to every problem is progress over perfection. One step forward, everyday. Mikki learned to see challenges not as roadblocks but as puzzles to be solved (and she so enjoyed doing puzzles!)

Mikki's parents also taught her to see the silver lining around the darkest cloud. Literally. They would take her to places where she got a clear view of rays coming out from dark clouds, or where she could point out the "bright glowing border" around the cloud. They encouraged her to focus on what she could control because what one focuses on, grows. They let her take small measures toward overcoming any challenge she faced. Mikki was taught to believe in herself and to never give up because a chapter was difficult, or training was tough, or the teacher was "not nice."

Understanding these lessons, Mikki began to develop her own ways of coping with challenges. When she faced difficulties at school, or had problems performing well in her extracurricular activities, she would take a deep breath and break down big problems into smaller, more manageable parts to tackle them one step at a time.

One evening, while doing her homework, Mikki struggled with a particularly tough math problem. She felt frustrated and wanted to give up. But then she remembered her parents' words- "What you focus on, grows." She changed her lens and went through the example problems, reworked the steps and finally solved it. In fact, she finished the exercise because she chose to focus on understanding the problem, and not simply finishing homework. She let out a delighted laugh and clapped happily for herself. Fighting and winning that small battle gave her a sense of accomplishment and pride.

Mikki also learned the importance of reaching out for help and realized that it was never a bad thing. But also knowing where and who to show her vulnerability to. Afterall one should not bleed in front of the sharks.When things got too difficult, she knew she could turn to her parents, teachers, or friends for support. She realized that asking for help wasn't a sign of weakness, but a way to learn and grow stronger. This understanding made her more confident and more supported to face new challenges.

Her positive attitude and resilience began to shine through in everything she did. When her basketball team lost a game, she would go through the highlights and understand what could be improved and practice. Mikki's friends, family, and loved ones all admired her for her sunshine spirit and her ability to bounce back from setbacks. Coping with challenges is especially important for children because it helps them build resilience and adaptability. Life is full of ups and downs, and learning to handle difficulties with courage and determination prepares children for the future because parents can't be omnipresent in their child's lives and they can't fight their battles for them. It teaches them to stay strong in the face of challenges and to keep moving forward, no matter what obstacles they meet. For Mikki, learning to cope with challenges made her a stronger and more confident person. She realized that every challenge she faced was an opportunity to learn something new and to grow. She began to see herself as a person on whom she can rely on. Her parents' love and support played a big role in this. They celebrated her efforts, not just her successes, and encouraged her to keep trying even when things were tough. They taught her that the journey was just as important as the destination and that every step forward was a victory in itself.

As the wheel of time turned, and life threw its curve balls at her, Mikki's ability to cope with challenges became one of her greatest strengths.

Story 13: The Trial(s) of Friendship

Friends are an essential part of our lives. They bring joy, share our secrets, and stand by us in times of need. However, when friends turn mean or into bullies, it can be one of the hardest challenges to face. We all rely on friends to have our backs, be our place of joy and solace, and look out for us.

In the first taste of betrayal from a friend that Mikki received, her best friend started dating the boy she liked, who was also her close friend. This hurt her deeply, and her entire friend group turned against her, calling her names (again) and cutting her off.

Mikki felt abandoned, isolated and heartbroken. "I don't understand why they're being so mean. I never did anything wrong to any of them. So why are they doing all this to me?" she cried one evening, tears streaming down her face. "They were my friends, and she knew I liked him. Why did she choose to not tell me first? Why am I made to feel bad for the things they have done?"

Her mother held her close, comforting her. Her daughter was heart broken for the first time, and there was nothing she could do other than feel helpless. "This too shall pass. Let the feeling stay tonight. Exhale. Tomorrow it will be a degree lesser. I love you!"

Days turned into weeks, and weeks into months. Mikki bravely faced each day, even though she felt alone. She had no friends in the new place, and her best friends back home had turned their backs on her. Yet, she never let bitterness take root in her heart. She continued to seek friends, share her heart, and be her own sweet self, hoping that one day things would get better. There was a lot of healing to do. She found that support in two people (who turned out to be bigger bullies later, but that's another story!)

Her resilience paid off. Slowly, she started making new friends in the new place. The first year in school wasn't easy. She accepted new ways to be outgoing while keeping her beliefs and values intact. She learnt to take jokes on herself, and learnt that it's important to shed skin. It's important to move with the change. Embrace change. Allow the change to shape, mould and carve one more beautifully. Permit the change to strengthen beliefs, expand thinking, and allow freshness to broaden the boundaries or mind.

One day, she received an unexpected message from one of her old friends that read- "I'm sorry for what happened. I was a lousy friend. Thank you for being you. Happy New Year!"

Mikki experienced many happy emotions at once and she replied back "Duffer! Happy New Year!" and they video called each other and caught up on time lost! They became close friends again, just like before.

However, her once best friend continued to stay aloof and indifferent. But Mikki accepted it with a quiet resolve. She had come to understand that if that friend valued Mikki as much as Mikki valued her, she would try to make amends with Mikki. And Mikki was willing to patiently wait for that day, or even accept that the day might never come.

She continues to be the fiercest friend for those she holds close to her heart.

She built up her confidence and courage after tackling this situation, but little did she know that another googly was waiting for her. Mikki faced a very tough time with her friends, which proved to be a big challenge in her life. This one time, she had a panic attack on a trip. Her roommate, whom she considered a dear friend, called upon other two friends and fought with her when she was in her most vulnerable state. Calling her names, ridiculing her, blaming her while she was recuperating from the panic attack. Mikki was hurt, embarrassed, isolated, bullied and abandoned by the very people who she once considered her close friends. She assumed that once back in town, she would take steps forward to heal herself.

But these 'friends' went back to school and spread nasty rumors about her vulnerable situation. They continued to shun her, speaking badly about her in their WhatsApp groups.

Despite this, Mikki remained dignified. She still greeted their mothers warmly, hugged them, talked to them, and wished them well on festivals. She showed the due respect that should be shown to elders. The beauty was that she never pretended any of it. It came from within.

"Why do you still talk to them, Mikki? Their daughters don't return a smile to me," her mother asked one day, concern etched on her face. "And they are still calling you names during practice. Being obnoxiously mean!"

Mikki looked up, her eyes shining with a quiet strength. "It's not the mothers' fault. You think they know how mean their daughters are being? Just because their daughters continue to be mean, I have to work on bouncing back. They have embarrassed and humiliated me by making my panic attack a joke with everyone I know. But see the bright side, none of my friends believed what they were told about me and they told me that they stand by me, and I should tell them how to manage a panic attack. You have taught me to be respectful to elders, no matter what. So I really like to hug them and ask them how they are. "

Her mother hugged her tightly, feeling a swell of pride.

<u>Story 14: Mikki's Moment of Strength</u>

One sunny afternoon, Mikki and her friends had the most wonderful playday. It was rare to have all her friends available at the same time, and this plan had been made rather in the spur of the moment. As they played hide-and-seek, one-minute pastry eating, chain-chain, corners, football, slides, and slime, the house was filled with laughter and joy. Mikki couldn't have been happier. "This is the best day ever!" she exclaimed, her face glowing with excitement. A few days later, however, tragedy struck. One of Mikki's dear friends, who had been joyfully playing with her on that wonderful last day they would spend together, passed away unexpectedly. The news hit Mikki hard, and she felt a deep sadness that she had never experienced before. She was so young but she had been suddenly thrown into one of the most emotionally demanding challenges. The loss of a loved one is difficult for anyone to cope with and Mikki felt utterly lost. She could not wrap her mind around the deeply sad thoughts in there and did not know how to continue ahead on the walk of life after her friend had so suddenly left her hand.

On their way back home, when grief was sitting like a heavy rock on Mikki's mind, she turned to her mother and said, "I'm glad all of us played together before this. It was one of the most fun days I had, and I'm glad she was a part of it."

When they returned home, Mikki curled up in the comforting embrace of her mother. She asked to see the photos from that day and as her mother went ahead to each new photo, Mikki recounted in a small voice some or the other fun memory that she had with her dearly departed friend from that day. As they ended on a lovely group photo, Mikki tenderly stroked the screen and seeing her friend's carefree laugh, said, "I will always remember this smile of hers."

Despite her grief, Mikki showed incredible maturity. She wanted to keep her friend's memory alive in her heart and in her actions. When her friend's sister returned to school, Mikki made it a point to meet her at the gate and walk her to class every day. During breaks, she talked to her, played with her, and chatted about school. She took care of the sister just like her friend would have.

Mikki also carried her friend's photograph in her bag and remembered her birthday. For the longest time, Mikki and her family continued to make a birthday invite for her and keep a return gift for her. It was their way of honoring her memory and keeping her spirit alive.

"I pray that she continues to laugh and smile wherever she is," Mikki said one evening, looking at the stars.

Mikki's ability to cope with the loss of her friend showed remarkable strength and compassion. She focused on the happy memories and found ways to support her friend's sister, showing that even in the face of great sadness, love and kindness can bring comfort and healing.

Mikki's journey through this difficult time teaches us that while losing a friend is incredibly hard, remembering the good times and being there for others can help us heal. By keeping her friend's memory alive in her heart and actions, Mikki turned her pain into a source of strength and compassion.

Life will always have its ups and downs, but with a healthy attitude and a loving heart, we can navigate even the toughest challenges. Mikki's story reminds us all that, no matter how dark things may seem, there is always a way to bring light back into our lives. Her resilience and kindness are a testament to the power of a positive attitude and the importance of cherishing the memories of those we love.

And now, as Mikki navigates life as a teenager, her mother, me, I find myself both proud and wistful.

Gone are the days when she clung to my hand, her laughter echoing through our home, and endless stories starting with "then do you know what happened…?!". Her world has expanded—friends, school, dreams, and secrets shared in hushed tones. I watch from the sidelines, a silent witness to her metamorphosis. Many time not knowingwhere to step in, and when to step- out.

It's bittersweet, this shift. She no longer rushes to tell me every detail of her day. Instead, she confides in friends, seeking their counsel. She says that I "will not understand", and she "needs time to process".And while my heart aches when she stumbles, I know she must learn to pick herself up, and find her time when she is ready to share. (Mostly after 11 pm!)

Our Mumma & Mahu lunch dates, once our sacred cocoon, are replaced withplans—sleepovers, movies, adventures beyond our walls. The once magical "mumma's touch" is now "let me revise and improve". I know she's not abandoning me; she's spreading her wings. And yet, there's a pang—the quiet house, the shut door, the empty kitchen sill where once she used to lie down while I used to cook.

But here's the twist: Mikkihas become my protector. My BFF. My go-to person to discuss things when I want to bounce ideas. She senses my moods, offers advice on how I should set boundaries with other, and gently nudges me to focus on what matters. She give me a patient ear when I am venting about relatives & family. The role reversal is both humbling and heartwarming. Scary at times too, because my lessons come back to me in ways I least expect.

Before the book ends, here is something from my thank-you scroll To all of you - Now that you know my world, also know that Mikki's laughter still echoes here. She still snuggles between her father and meand talks till we have to beg her to stop. Our monthly binge-watching of "old" movies continues. Infact now we say the dialogues. Her hugs are tighter. Her jokes are funnier. Her moods are scarier too. Her wisdom guides me, and her love keeps our home warm.. Life, in all its messy complexity, continues to make us laugh while holding hands and leaning on each other. I Thank you for reading the book, hoping that you enjoyed reading it as much as I enjoyed sharing my my stories with you

To Manav – I Love you so much. The lines are for you, "Life is a road and I wanna keep going. Love is a river and I wanna keep flowing. Life is a road now and forever a wonderful journey. I will be there when the world stops turning, I will be there when the storm is through, at the end I want to be standing at the beginning with you!" (Song by Donna Lewis & Richard Marx titles At the beginning of the movie Anastasia)

To Mikki – Thank you for inspiring me to do this. This book is because that day you didn't give up and kept going. Stay like that. One's biggest battle is to fight one's demons. Not others. I do want you to know that life will always has its momentsready to surprise you. Moments that will test you, push you, and tempt you. People will come and go, and so will good and bad times. You will try new things. You should. Sometimes it will work, and sometimes it won't. Either way, own your stuff.. And make it better. You will get hurt, ditched, cheated, and backstabbed. And similarly you will get loved, protected, and doted upon too. As your world broadens, you will meet people who will seed self-doubt, or tell what you can or cannot do. In these moments, my love, I hope you find the answer in these stories to know that you can do anything when you put your mid and heart to it. Love moves mountainsThe only person who should validate you- is you. I urge you to stand tall in your truth. Cut the frills. Say no. Don't worry about "what the world would say", because "the world" will talk anyways. In the larger context of the universe, there is nothing right or wrong.What felt right once, can feel wrong later too.Sometimes you will be the hunter and sometimes you will be the hunted. Life is contextual.What will remain constant is your trust in her inner compass. One day at a time. In the worries of tomorrow, don't miss today. You owe it to yourself to be the best version of yourself. Your father and I believe in you and love you. Super proud of you!

So in the beginning, I had written that sometimes the bravest act is to let our stories breathe allowing them to find their way back home. At the end of the book I want to rephrase the line to sometimes the bravest act is not just letting our stories breathe but allowing them to intertwine with others. Intentionally fall in love with the moments.

Thank you for reading, and welcome to my world of You, Me & Mikki!

Verses Kindler Publication

Reach us through our website -
https://www.verseskindlerpublication.com/
For more information visit our Instagram or Facebook page.